THIS WALKER BOOK BELONGS TO:

_____

_____

_____

_____

First published 1991 by Walker Books Ltd
87 Vauxhall Walk, London SE11 5HJ

This edition published 2001

2 4 6 8 10 9 7 5 3

© 1991 Nick Butterworth

This book has been typeset in Times

Printed in Hong Kong

British Library Cataloguing in Publication Data:
a catalogue record for this book is available from the British Library

ISBN 0-7445-8251-2

MY GRANDMA IS WONDERFUL

Nick Butterworth

WALKER BOOKS
AND SUBSIDIARIES
LONDON · BOSTON · SYDNEY

My grandma is wonderful.

She always buys
the biggest ice-creams …

and she never,
ever loses at noughts
and crosses …

and she knows
all about nature …

and she's brilliant
at untying knots ...

and she's always
on your side when
things go wrong …

and she makes
the most fantastic
clothes …

and when you're ill,
she can make you forget
that you don't feel well ...

and she can scream
really loudly …

and she has marvellous hearing …

and no matter where
you are, she always
has what you need
in her handbag.

It's great to have a
grandma like mine.

She's wonderful!

NICK BUTTERWORTH says of **My Grandma Is Wonderful**, "I wonder how much time I spent as a boy singing the praises of my family. My grandpa could make *anything* out of *anything*. My gran was the best friend anyone could ever wish for. My dad was little short of Superman and my mum ... well, perhaps she actually *was* Wonderwoman! It's heartening to know that children feel the same today as I did then. Especially my own two!"

Nick Butterworth has worked as a graphic designer, television presenter, magazine editor and cartoon-strip illustrator, and has written and illustrated many successful children's books as well. These include the Walker titles *My Dad Is Brilliant*, *My Mum Is Fantastic*, *My Grandpa Is Amazing*, *Making Faces*, *Jack the Carpenter and His Friends* and *Jill the Farmer and Her Friends*. Nick is also the creator of the bestselling *Percy the Park Keeper* series.

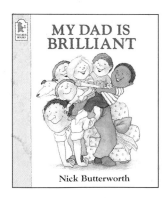

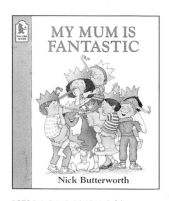

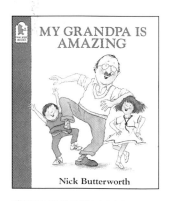

ISBN 0-7445-8248-2 (pb)   ISBN 0-7445-8249-0 (pb)   ISBN 0-7445-8250-4 (pb)